For Hannah

First published in the UK 2020 by Macmillan Children's Books
an imprint of Pan Macmillan
The Smithson, 6 Briset Street, London EC1M 5NR
Associated companies throughout the world
www.panmacmillan.com

ISBN (PB): 978-1-5098-2748-0

1 3 5 7 9 8 6 4 2

A CIP catalogue record for this book is available from the British Library.

Printed in China

# Sue Hendra & Paul Linnet

# EGG

MACMILLAN CHILDREN'S BOOKS

egg . . .    egg . . .    egg . . .

egg . . .          egg . . .          egg . . .

egg?

egg.

egg.

egg?

egg!

eeeeegg...

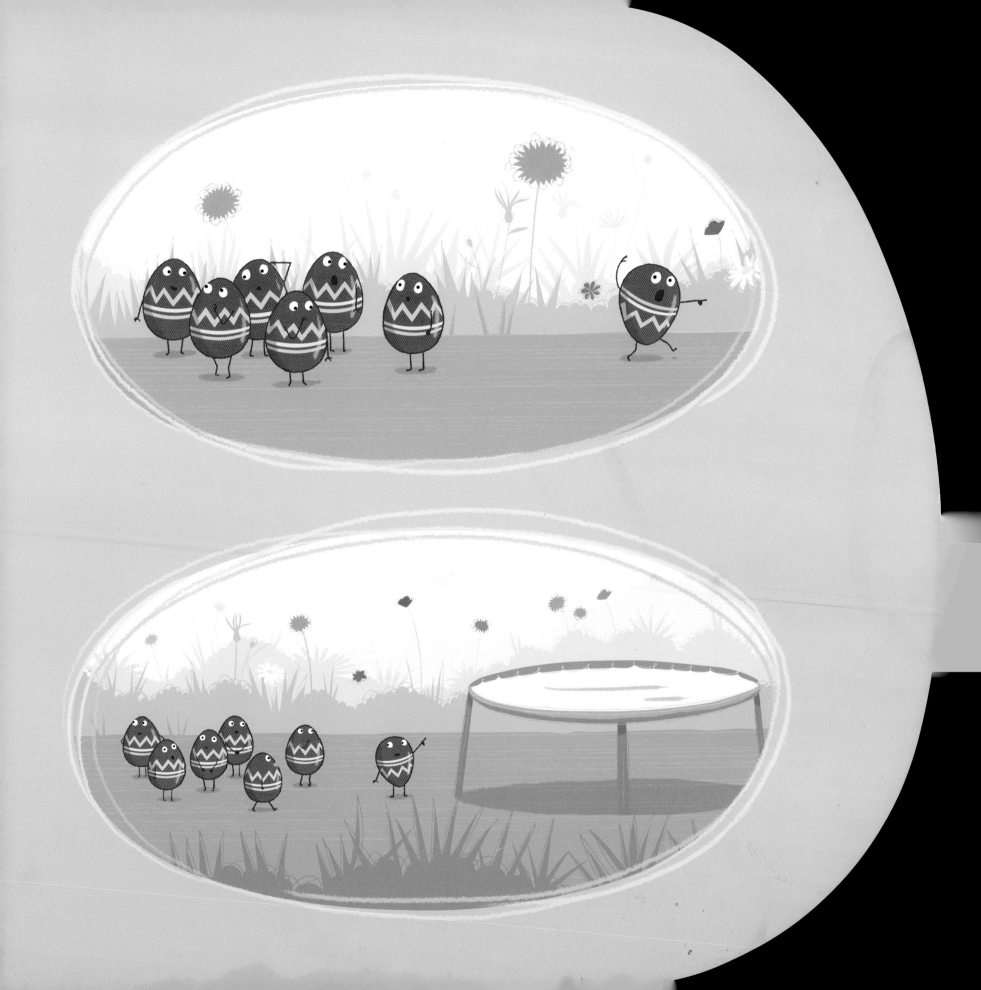

eggs.